The Four Princesses
and other poems

Compiled by Tig Thomas

Miles KeLLy

First published in 2010 by Miles Kelly Publishing Ltd
Harding's Barn, Bardfield End Green, Thaxted, Essex, CM6 3PX, UK

2 4 6 8 10 9 7 5 3 1

Editorial Director Belinda Gallagher

Art Director Jo Cowan

Assistant Editor Claire Philip

Designer Joe Jones

Junior Designer Kayleigh Allen

Production Manager Elizabeth Collins

Reprographics Stephan Davis, Ian Paulyn

ISBN 978-1-84810-366-5

Printed in China

British Library Cataloguing-in-Publication Data
A catalogue record for this book is available from the British Library

ACKNOWLEDGEMENTS

The publishers would like to thank Kirsten Wilson for
the illustrations she contributed to this book.

All other artwork from the Miles Kelly Artwork Bank

Made with paper from a sustainable forest

www.mileskelly.net
info@mileskelly.net

www.factsforprojects.com

Self-publish your
children's book

buddingpress.co.uk

Contents

The Music of your Voice

A vase upon the mantelpiece,
   A ship upon the sea,
A goat upon a mountain-top
   Are much the same to me;
But when you mention melon jam,
   Or picnics by the creek,
Or apple pies, or pantomimes,
   I love to hear you speak.

Magna Carta an important document signed by the King of England in 1215

The date of Magna Carta or
  The doings of the Dutch,
Or capes, or towns, or verbs, or nouns
  Do not excite me much;
But when you mention motor rides –
  Down by the sea for choice
Or chasing games, or chocolates,
  I love to hear your voice.

C J Dennis

5

A Witch's Spell

Fillet of a fenny snake,
In the cauldron boil and bake;
Eye of newt, and toe of frog,
Wool of bat, and tongue of dog,

Adder's fork, and blind-worm's sting,
Lizard's leg, and howlet's wing,
For a charm of powerful trouble,
Like a hell-broth boil and bubble.

Double, double toil and trouble;
Fire burn and cauldron bubble. . .

Cool it with a baboon's blood
Now the spell is thick and good.

William Shakespeare

An Elf Singing

An **Elf** sat on a twig,
He was not very big,
He sang a little song,
He did not think it wrong;
But he was on a Wizard's ground,
Who hated all sweet sound.

Elf, Elf,

Take care of yourself,
He's coming behind you,
To seize you and bind you
And stifle your song.
The Wizard! the Wizard!
He changes his shape

In crawling along,
An ugly old ape,
A poisonous lizard,
A spotted spider,
A wormy glider,

The Wizard! the Wizard!
He's up on the bough,
He'll bite through your gizzard,
He's close to you now!

The **Elf** went on with his song,
It grew more clear and strong,
It lifted him in the air,
He floated singing away,
With rainbows in his hair;
While the Wizard-worm from his creep
Made a sudden leap,
Fell down into a hole,
And, ere his magic word he could say,
Was eaten up by a Mole.

William Allingham

There were Three Sisters

There were three sisters fair and bright,
Jennifer gentle and rosemary,
And they three loved one valiant knight.
As the dew flies over the mulberry tree.

The eldest sister let him in,
Jennifer gentle and rosemary,
And barred the door with a silver pin,
As the dew flies over the mulberry tree.

The second sister made his bed,
Jennifer gentle and rosemary,
And placed soft pillows under his head,
As the dew flies over the mulberry tree.

The youngest sister, fair and bright,
    Jennifer gentle and rosemary,
Was resolved for to wed with this valiant knight,
    As the dew flies over the mulberry tree.

"And if you can answer questions three,
    Jennifer gentle and rosemary,
O then, fair maid, I will marry with thee.
    As the dew flies over the mulberry tree.

"What is louder than a horn,
    Jennifer gentle and rosemary,
And what is sharper than a thorn?"
    *As the dew flies over the
        mulberry tree.*

"Thunder is louder than a horn,
  Jennifer gentle and rosemary,
And hunger is sharper than a thorn."
  As the dew flies over the mulberry tree.

"What is broader than the way,
  Jennifer gentle and rosemary,
And what is deeper than the sea?"
  As the dew flies over the mulberry tree.

"Love is broader than the way,
  Jennifer gentle and rosemary,
And hell is deeper than the sea."
  As the dew flies over the mulberry tree.

"And now, fair maid, I will marry thee."

Anonymous

Boy-Dreams

I was a Pirate once,
A blustering fellow with scarlet sash,
A ready cutlass and language rash;
From a ship with a rum-filled water tank
I made the enemy walk the plank;
I marooned a man on an island bare,
And seized his wife by her long, dark hair;
Took treasure, such heaps of it! — Wealth untold
— Bright bars of silver and chunks of gold!
Till my ship was choked to the decks with pelf,
And no one dare touch it except myself
And my black flag waved to the tearing breeze,
And I was the terror of all the seas!

Pelf riches

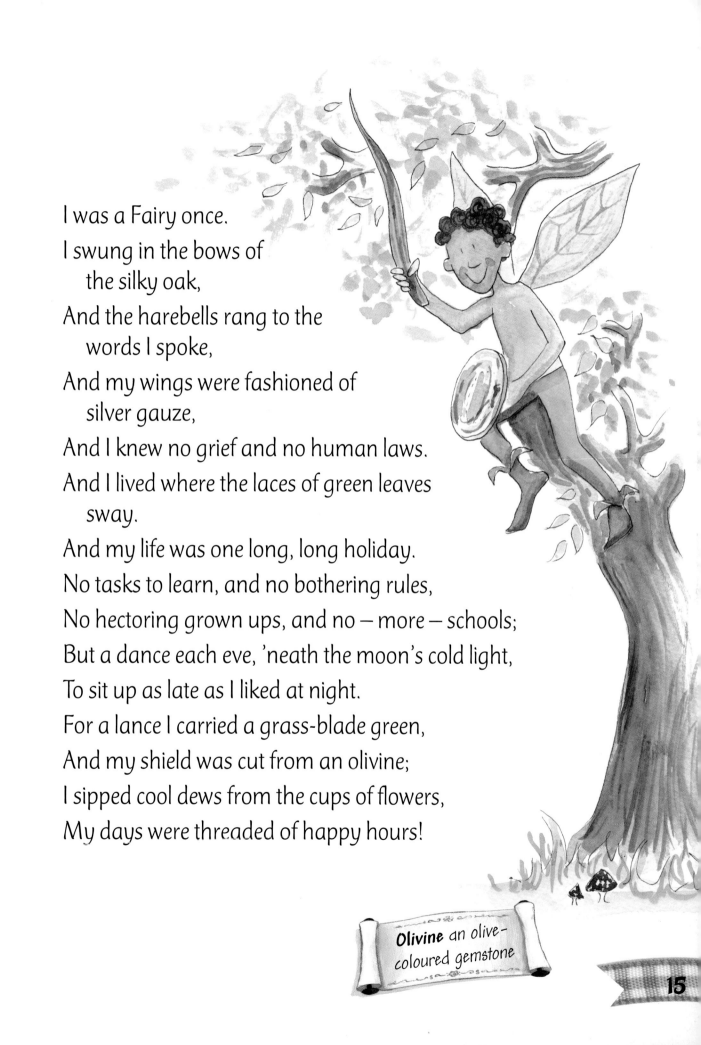

I was a Fairy once.
I swung in the bows of
    the silky oak,
And the harebells rang to the
    words I spoke,
And my wings were fashioned of
    silver gauze,
And I knew no grief and no human laws.
And I lived where the laces of green leaves
    sway.
And my life was one long, long holiday.
No tasks to learn, and no bothering rules,
No hectoring grown ups, and no – more – schools;
But a dance each eve, 'neath the moon's cold light,
To sit up as late as I liked at night.
For a lance I carried a grass-blade green,
And my shield was cut from an olivine;
I sipped cool dews from the cups of flowers,
My days were threaded of happy hours!

Olivine an olive-
coloured gemstone

I was a Merman once.
In the gloom of the amber-tinted seas,
With the brown tang clinging about my knees,
With a coral house, and a crab to ride,
Who pranced, and who ambled from side to side;
I wooed a Mermaid with emerald hair,
Dragged the fierce sea serpent from out his lair,
With his flaming tongue and his awful might,
And I slew him – easy – in open fight!
I had strings of pearls, white as frozen milk,
That were strung for me on *sea-spider's silk*;
And I never pined for the upper skies,
Whose blue came down in the dead men's eyes,
Drowned men with the salt on their blackened lips,
Who slid, drifting in, from the wrecks of ships;
But I took the gold from the belts of all,
To pave the road to my coral hall.

Tang *a coarse seaweed*

I was a Hunter once,

And I trapped and stalked in a pathless wood,

And the talk of the wild things understood.

With my leather leggings and hat of brown.

I tracked the elk and the redskin down;

    Slew a grizzly bear in a mountain cave,

      And tweaked the nose of an Indian brave.

      Ere I shot the rapids in birch canoe –

     For there was nothing I could not do.

    There was naught I did not dare or enjoy,

In the magic world of a dreaming boy!

M Forrest

17

The Four Princesses

Four Princesses lived in a Green Tower –
   A Bright Green Tower in the middle of the sea;
And no one could think – oh, no one could think –
   Who the Four Princesses could be.

One looked to the North, and one to the South,
   And one to the East, and one to the West;
They were all so pretty, so very pretty,
   You could not tell which was the prettiest.

Their curls were golden – their eyes were blue,
   And their voices were sweet as a silvery bell;
And four white birds around them flew,
   But where they came from – who
      could tell?

Oh, who could tell? For no one knew,
 And not a word could you hear them say,
  But the sound of their singing, like church bells ringing,
   Would sweetly float as they passed away.

    For under the sun, and under the stars,
     They often sailed on the distant sea;
    Then in their Green Tower and Roses bower
     They lived again – a mystery.

Kate Greenaway

Oh! Dear!

Oh! Dear! What can the matter be?
Dear! Dear! What can the matter be?
Oh! Dear! What can the matter be?
Johnny's so long at the fair.

He promised he'd buy me a fairing should please me,
And then for a kiss, oh! He vowed he would tease me,
He promised he'd bring me a bunch of blue ribbons
To tie up my bonny brown hair.

And it's oh! Dear! What can the matter be?
Dear! Dear! What can the matter be?
Oh! Dear! What can the matter be?
Johnny's so long at the fair.

Fairing a gift bought at a fair for a sweetheart

He promised he'd bring me a basket of posies,
A garland of lilies, a garland of roses,
A little straw hat, to set off the blue ribbons
That tie up my bonny brown hair.

And it's oh! Dear! What can the matter be?
Dear! Dear! What can the matter be?
Oh! Dear! What can the matter be?
Johnny's so long at the fair.

Anonymous

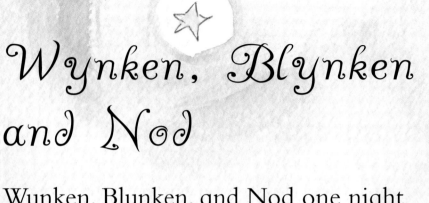

Wynken, Blynken and Nod

Wynken, Blynken, and Nod one night
Sailed off in a wooden shoe –
Sailed on river of crystal light,
Into a sea of dew.
"Where are you going, and what do you wish?"
The old moon asked the three.
"We have come to fish for the herring-fish
That live in this beautiful sea;
Nets of silver and gold have we!"
Said Wynken,
Blynken,
And Nod.

The old moon laughed and sang a song,
As they rocked in the wooden shoe,
And the wind that sped them all night long
Ruffled the waves of dew.
The little stars were the herring-fish
That lived in that beautiful sea –
"Now cast your nets wherever you wish
But never a feared are we";
So cried the stars to the fishermen three:
Wynken,
Blynken,
And Nod.

All night long their nets they threw

To the stars in the twinkling foam –

Then down from the skies came the wooden
    shoe,

Bringing the fishermen home;

'Twas all so pretty a sail, it seemed

As if it could not be,

And some folks thought 'twas a dream they'd
    dreamed

Of sailing that beautiful sea

But I shall name you the fishermen three:

Wynken,

Blynken,

And Nod.

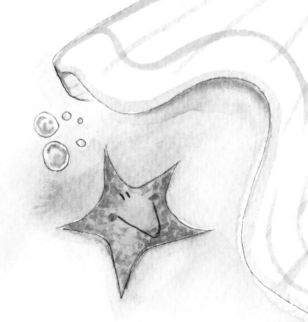

Wynken and Blynken are two little eyes,
And Nod is a little head,
And the wooden shoe that sailed the skies
Is a wee one's trundle-bed.
So shut your eyes while mother sings
Of wonderful sights that be,
And you shall see the beautiful things
As you rock on the misty sea,
Where the old shoe rocked the fishermen three:
Wynken,
Blynken,
And Nod.

Eugene Field

A Fairy's Song

Where the bee sucks, there suck I;

In the cowslip's bell I lie;

There I couch when owls do cry

On the bat's back I do fly

After summer, merrily:

Merrily, merrily shall I live now,

Under the blossom that hangs on the bough.

William Shakespeare

Couch lie

Queen Mab

A little fairy comes at night,
Her eyes are blue, her hair is brown,
With silver spots upon her wings,
And from the moon she flutters down.

She has a little silver wand,
And when a good child goes to bed
She waves her wand from right to left,
And makes a circle round its head.

And then it dreams of pleasant things,
Of fountains filled with fairy fish,
And trees that bear delicious fruit
And bow their branches at a wish.

Of arbours filled with dainty scents
From lovely flowers that never fade;
Bright flies that glitter in the sun,
And glow-worms shining in the shade:

And talking birds with gifted tongues,
For singing songs and telling tales,
And pretty dwarfs to show the way
Through fairy hills and fairy dales.

But when a bad child goes to bed,
From left to right she weaves her rings,
And then it dreams all through the night
Of only ugly, horrid things!

Then lions come with glaring eyes,
And tigers growl, a dreadful noise,
And ogres draw their cruel knives,
To shed the blood of girls and boys.

Then stormy waves rush on to drown,
Or raging flames come scorching round,
Fierce dragons hover in the air,
And serpents crawl along the ground.

Then wicked children wake and weep,
And wish the long black gloom away;
But good ones love the dark, and find
The night as pleasant as the day.

Thomas Hood

A Prince

A daring prince, of the realm Rangg Dhune,
Once went up in a big balloon
That caught and stuck on the horns of the moon,
And he hung up there till next day noon —
When all at once he exclaimed, "**Hoot-toot!**"
And then came down in his parachute.

James Whitcomb Riley

Climbing

High up in the apple tree climbing I go,
With the sky above me, the Earth below.
Each branch is the step of a wonderful stair
Which leads to the town I see shining up there.

Climbing, climbing, higher and higher,
The branches blow and I see a spire,
The gleam of a turret, the glint of a dome,
All sparkling and bright, like white sea foam.

On and on, from bough to bough,
    The leaves are thick, but I push my way through;
Before, I have always had to stop,
But today I am sure I shall reach the top.

Today to the end of the marvellous stair,
Where those glittering pinacles flash in the air!
Climbing, climbing, higher I go,
With the sky close above me, the earth far below.

Amy Lowell

Terence McDiddler

Terence McDiddler,
The three-stringed fiddler,
Can charm, if you please,
The fish from the seas.

Anonymous

A Fairy in Armour

He put his acorn helmet on;
It was plumed of the silk of the
    thistle down;
The corslet plate that guarded
    his breast
Was once the wild bee's golden vest;
His cloak, of a thousand mingled dyes,
Was formed of the wings of butterflies;
His shield was the shell of a lady-bird green,
Studs of gold on a ground of green;
And the quivering lance which he brandished
    bright,
Was the sting of a wasp he had slain in fight.

Joseph Rodman Drake

A Big Shoe

Said little Sue
To little Pete,
"I can't see you,
For your big feet."

Said little Pete
To little Sue
"'Tis not my feet,
'Tis but my shoe."

Anonymous

Sea Shell

Sea Shell, Sea Shell,

Sing me a song, O Please!
A song of ships, and sailor men,
And parrots, and tropical trees,
Of islands lost in the Spanish Main
Which no man ever may find again,
Of fishes and corals under the waves,
And seahorses stabled in great green caves.

Sea Shell, Sea Shell,

Sing of the things you know so well.

Amy Lowell

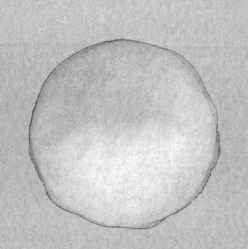

From *The Gipsies*

The fairy beam upon you,

The stars to glisten on you,

A moon of light

In the noon of night,

Till the firedrake hath o'er-gone you.

The wheel of fortune guide you,

The boy with the bow beside you

Run aye in the way

Till the bird of day

And the luckier lot betide you.

Ben Jonson

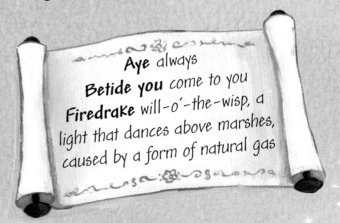

Aye always
Betide you come to you
Firedrake will-o'-the-wisp, a
light that dances above marshes,
caused by a form of natural gas

Index of First Lines